GO NICK JR. DiEGO GO!™

Diego's Safari Rescue

adapted by Ligiah Villalobos

based on the original teleplay by Ligiah Villalobos

illustrated by Alex Maher

SCHOLASTIC INC.
New York Toronto London Auckland Sydney
Mexico City New Delhi Hong Kong Buenos Aires

¡Hola! I'm Diego. I'm an Animal Rescuer. This is my sister Alicia, and this is Baby Jaguar. We're visiting the Serengeti in Africa to help our friend Juma rescue the elephants!

Juma says that a long time ago, the Serengeti in Africa had lots and lots of elephants. Do you see all of the elephants? *¡Sí!* There they are. All of the animals loved the elephants—except for one mosquito who found a magic wand and changed herself into a magician.

The magician didn't like elephants, so she used her magic wand to turn them into giant rocks!

Juma says there's a magic drum that can break the magician's spell. It's hidden in a cave on top of the tallest mountain. Do you see the tallest mountain? *¡Sí!* That's the tallest mountain. And there's the cave.

We'll need something that can get us to the top of that mountain. Who can help? Rescue Pack! To activate Rescue Pack, say *"¡Actívate!"*

Rescue Pack can transform into anything we need: a boat, roller skates, or a hot-air balloon. What can fly us all the way to the top of the tallest mountain? *¡Sí!* A hot-air balloon!

Rescue Pack transformed into a hot-air balloon. *Bien hecho*, Rescue Pack! Now we can go find the magic drum! Come on!

We made it to the cave. And look! There's an elephant! Her name is Erin. She says she came to the cave to hide from the magician and protect the magic drum. Do you see the magic drum? *¡Sí!* There it is!

Now that we've found the magic drum, we can go rescue the elephants who turned into rocks! Our special camera, Click, will help us find out where they are. Say "Click!"

Click says we'll have to go through the dry forest and across the lake to get to the giant rocks so we can break the spell and rescue the elephants. *¡Al rescate!* To the rescue!

We made it to the dry forest, but the trees are blocking our way. Erin the Elephant says she can use her trunk to pull the trees out of the way. Elephants have superstrong trunks!

Will you help Erin the Elephant pull the trees out of the way? Great! Make elephant trunks with your arms, and pull, pull, pull!

Great job pulling like an elephant. Now the trees aren't blocking our way! And look! Do you see the giraffes? They look different, don't they? *¡Sí!* The magician made their necks really short.

Juma says that maybe the magic drum can help us make their necks long again. Will you beat the magic drum with us? *¡Excelente!* Put your hands out in front of you, and drum, drum, drum!

It worked! The magic drum made the giraffes' necks long again! The giraffes say thank you. Let's keep going so we can rescue the elephants!

Uh-oh! I hear a lion roaring! Alicia says that elephants are afraid of lions. But elephants can scare away lions by stomping their feet very loudly. Let's help Erin the Elephant scare away the lion. Stomp with your feet! Stomp, stomp, stomp!

Yay! We helped Erin the Elephant scare away the lion. And we made it to the lake. The lake is very deep, but we've got to find a way to get across it!

Erin the Elephant says elephants love to swim. She says she can get us across! Will you help Erin the Elephant swim across the lake? *¡Excelente!* Put your arms out in front of you, and swim, swim, swim!

We made it across the lake. *¡Gracias!* Thanks for helping!

Hey, look! Do you see the zebras and hippos? Do they look different? *¡Sí!* The magician took away the zebras' stripes and made the hippos really small.

Juma thinks the magic drum can help them. Let's beat the magic drum! Put your hands out in front of you, and drum, drum, drum!

The magic drum worked!
The zebras got their stripes
back, and the hippos are big
again! Let's keep going so we
can break the spell and save all
of the elephants.

We made it to the rocks. Those
are the elephants we need to save!
Oh, no! There's the magician! She
turned Erin the Elephant into a rock!

We've got to use the magic drum to unfreeze all of the elephants! Drum with us! Put your hands out in front of you, and drum, drum, drum!

Hooray! We turned the rocks back into elephants!

Let's use Rescue Rope to lasso the magic wand away from the magician. Great!

The magician turned into a mosquito.

The mosquito says she missed being a mosquito and will never do mean things again. Look! She's flying away!

Erin the Elephant says she's so happy to see all of her elephant friends again!
¡Misión cumplida! Rescue complete! You are great at rescuing animals! *¡Hasta luego!* See you soon!

Did you know?

Dinnertime

Big, Big, Big!

Elephants are the biggest land animals in all of Africa. They're as heavy as twelve pick-up trucks!

Elephants love to eat lots of things, like tree branches, fruit, and grass. They spend up to sixteen hours a day looking for food because they're hungry all the time!

Clean-up Time

Elephants can fill up their trunks with water and then squirt their backs with it! It's an easy way to take a quick shower!

Ear Fans

Fast Going

Elephants are very big, but it doesn't slow them down. They can run really fast!

Elephants have big, flat ears that they flap back and forth and use like fans to cool off!

Diego is headed to Africa for a safari! But someone has turned all of the elephants into rocks! Join Diego on an exciting safari rescue mission as he saves the elephants and meets all kinds of other animals along the way.

Look for more books about Go, Diego, Go! at your favorite store!

Diego's Wolf Pup Rescue

A Humpback Whale Tale

Diego and Papi to the Rescue

Diego Saves the Sloth!

Visit nickjr.com for more **Go, Diego, Go!** games, crafts, and activities!

www.nickjr.com

SCHOLASTIC
www.scholastic.com

This edition is available for distribution only through the school market.

Look for Nick Jr.
Books in Spanish

ISBN-13: 978-0-545-00968-3
ISBN-10: 0-545-00968-5   **$3.99 US**
50399

EAN
9 780545 009683